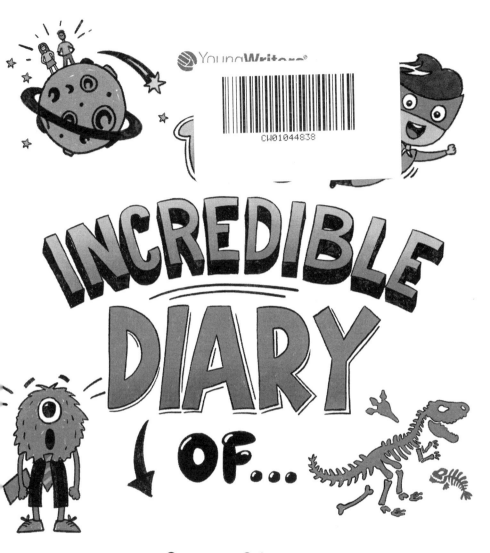

INCREDIBLE DIARY OF...

Super Stories

Edited By Byron Tobolik

First published in Great Britain in 2023 by:

Young Writers
Remus House
Coltsfoot Drive
Peterborough
PE2 9BF
Telephone: 01733 890066
Website: www.youngwriters.co.uk

Printed and bound in the UK by BookPrintingUK
Website: www.bookprintinguk.com
YB0551R

FOREWORD

Dear Diary,

You will never guess what I did today! Shall I tell you? Some primary school pupils wrote some diary entries and I got to read them, and they were EXCELLENT!

Here at Young Writers we created some bright and funky worksheets along with fun and fabulous (and free) resources to help spark ideas and get inspiration flowing. And it clearly worked because WOW!! I can't believe the adventures I've been reading about. Real people, make believe people, dogs and unicorns, even objects like pencils all feature and these diaries all have one thing in common – they are JAM-PACKED with imagination, all squeezed into 100 words!

Here at Young Writers we want to pass our love of the written word onto the next generation and what better way to do that than to celebrate their writing by publishing it in a book! It sets their work free from homework books and notepads and puts it where it deserves to be – **OUT IN THE WORLD!**

Each awesome author in this book should be super proud of themselves, and now they've got proof of their imagination, their ideas and their creativity in black and white, to look back on in years to come!

CONTENTS

Lady Katherine Leveson CE School, Knowle

Daniel Block (8)	62
Harry Hamer (9)	63
Holly Smith (9)	64
Eadie Hopkins Bird (9)	65
Logan Jackson-Foster (9)	66
Kai Timms (9)	67
Lucy Faithful-Eagles (8)	68
Aaron Blackmore-Wright (9)	69

Lycee International de Londres, Wembley

Dienaba Drame (10)	70
Sixtine Marais (9)	71
Lucile Tse (10)	72
Ayleen Djadel (9)	73
Koursami Nasour (10)	74
Giacomo Galieti (11)	75
Violet Le Junter-Sleath (8)	76
Malo Laplanche Galton (11)	77
Tara Tondriaux-Gautier (10)	78
Noah Wiseman (10)	79
Gabriel Chevalier (11)	80
Olivier Lo Dromer (10)	81
Romy Pourkauoos (10)	82
Zoe Guichard Polese (10)	83
Chloé Charrey (9)	84
Abibah Ka (9)	85
Ilhan Boulier (11)	86

Miers Court Primary School, Rainham

Flynn Rider (8)	87
Chloe Terry (8)	88
Louie Kellow (8)	89
Tanya Chikore (9)	90
Harry Harris (9)	91
Dennis Trice (9)	92
Ivy Conafray (8)	93
Avani Upple (9)	94

Jack Weeks (8)	95
Saul Lewis (9)	96
Olivia Ranger (9)	97
Jack Dodd (9)	98
Alyshba Bamitale (9)	99
Eleanor Searle (8)	100
Elena Mennell (8)	101
Lara Taylor (9)	102
Pyper Harris (9)	103
Rose Tingley (9)	104
Ella Wolff (9)	105
Cameron Tharp (9)	106
Rose Esme Collins (8)	107
Alfie Weeks (8)	108
Dariola Sulu (8)	109
Josh Thomas (8)	110
Riley Brown (8)	111
Jack Barber (8)	112
Joseph Hart (8)	113
Katie Keohane (8)	114
Ellie Libbeter (9)	115
Joel Olateju (9)	116
Sienna Lynch (9)	117
Lila Stockdale (9)	118
Maya Cockerell (8)	119
Ashton Bell (9)	120
Sienna-Sydney Dennis (8)	121
Sophia Bannister (9)	122
Saskia Bartos (8)	123
Eden-Rose Robson (8)	124
Nancy Noy (9)	125
Freddie-Ray Kehoe (8)	126
James Craddock (8)	127
Ellie Pinkney (9)	128
Isobel Clint (8)	129
Josh Sands (9)	130
George Baldwin (8)	131
Leila Ware (8)	132

St Andrew's Heddon-On-The-Wall CE Primary School, Heddon On The Wall

Adam Coates (9)	133
Belle Todd (9)	134
Henry Sanderson (10)	135
Finn Cassidy (10)	136
Isabella McLean (9)	137
Aaron Johnson (10)	138
Jacob Jude (10)	139
Freya Wilson (9)	140
Frazer Blake (10)	141
Austin Wilkinson Martin (10)	142
Molly Gray (10)	143
Ella Griffiths (10)	144
Chloe Loughead (10)	145
Archie Batey (9)	146
Sofia Robson (10)	147
Charlie Ellis (9)	148
Ethan Grieves (9)	149
Olivia Watson (10)	150

The Mill Academy, Worsbrough Bridge

Elena Swiderska (11)	151
Harry Burton (10)	152
Reuben Rooke (7)	153
Madison Townhill (6)	154
Lyla Maggie Dawson (8)	155
Emily Holden (6)	156
Katie Townhill (6)	157
Harper Burkinshaw (7)	158
Caleb Burkinshaw (6)	159

Wycliffe Prep School, Stonehouse

Niamh Pettingell (10)	160
Lumi Robertson (9)	161
Edward Hill (9)	162
Dylan Bushell (10)	163
Lewis Sandison (10)	164
Frank Carter (10)	165
Sammy Hughes (10)	166
Tay Bigger (10)	167
Brandon Lovewell (10)	168

THE STORIES

The Day Jerald Was Frightened

Dear Diary,

I was sitting on my bed when my phone got a notification. I went to get my phone. Suddenly, it started to talk! It shouted, "You can't get me!" and then it started to run out of the door.

I shouted to the phone, "I don't care because I just ordered an iPhone 14!"

"Oh no you didn't, because I cancelled the order, you big, fat dummy! Didn't you get the email? Oh, that's right. I am your phone!" shouted the phone.

"How can I get you back?" I asked.

"I am never coming back!" shouted the phone.

Alivia Curtis (8)

Cheddar Grove Primary School, Bedminster Down

The IPhone Came To Life

Dear Diary,

One stormy night, a mysterious phone got hit by a lightning strike. It happened in the Woods of Miracles and suddenly, eyes popped open and legs jumped out! It was crazy because arms sprung out of nowhere. A mouth materialised and a big nose. The iPhone thought to himself, *am I alive?*

He then wandered around until he found the lights of the city. "How am I going to get down there?" he asked himself. Also, there were like loads of elephants stacked, if that's what they're called. Luckily, he safely got down. Hooray! Off to bed now.

Rudi Daniel (8)

Cheddar Grove Primary School, Bedminster Down

Two Girls Turn Into Superheroes

Dear Diary,

Today was crazy and unbelievable. Me and Kate were going to school really peacefully and then it was already break. The teacher said we didn't have to do work and we didn't have to go to school, so we went home. Kate climbed over the fence and she said that we should play. I agreed, but suddenly I got struck by lightning. I started to fly, then teleport and became invisible. I figured out that I had powers and so did Kate. Everyone got powers as well. Everyone all lived happily ever after. Goodbye, see you tomorrow, bye.

Iola Jones (8)

Cheddar Grove Primary School, Bedminster Down

Milly's Lovely Day!

Dear Diary,

Today, I went to Spain. When I got there, I had some yummy sushi for breakfast. Then I went swimming in the clear, blue water for one hour. Also, my grandma and grandad live here, so we got to see them in person instead of calling or FaceTiming. In the afternoon, we went to an Italian restaurant and had some pasta. Then we went to the pub that had kid-friendly cocktails. My parents had a couple of beers. Don't tell!

Finally, we passed out and fell asleep and had amazing dreams. Night!

From Remi Ann Davidson.

Remi Ann Davidson (7)

Cheddar Grove Primary School, Bedminster Down

Super Teddy 2.96

Dear Diary,

I'm alive and I can talk and walk. None of the other teddies can, but I can! I've overheard a human talking about a terrible error in the teddy-making machine. I think that's how I came out like this. Today, a caterpillar named Little Johnny was giving me a tour of the factory when I spotted a teddy on the edge of a washing machine. They were about to fall. Quickly, I used tape which stuck to them and stopped them from falling. Little Johnny gave me a medal. I am a hero.

Lots of love,

2.96.

Norah Kebby (8)

Cheddar Grove Primary School, Bedminster Down

The Space Extravaganza

Dear Diary,

What I'm about to tell you is mind-boggling. In fact, it will even knock your socks off! But there's one thing, you mustn't say a word to anyone. And I know what you're about to say. No, you can't tell your dog. So, as I remember, it was yesterday that this happened and I know you won't believe me but here it is either way. I went to outer space! Here's how... I oddly found a cave.

As I went in, all of a sudden, there was a flash of light, and as I looked around, stars floated...

Rosie Gribble (11)

Cheddar Grove Primary School, Bedminster Down

The Special Ones

Hi, my name is Amithist and this is my friend, Bananas. We never knew we had powers until last week. We were camping on a sunny day and Bananas got in the pool. She was mad because the pool was too cold. Then suddenly, it was hot and I got mad because the pool was too hot. But again, the pool turned cold. Two people next door were intrigued, and so were we. So we started experimenting and by the time we finished, we knew we had powers. The men were experimenting on us. They got our blood, that's all.

Lilly Hubbard (9) & Avanna Brown (8)
Cheddar Grove Primary School, Bedminster Down

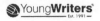
Legoland

Dear Diary,

Today is my birthday and I feel thankful because my mum and dad said yes to Legoland, which was £500. I was awake very early because we stayed in the Legoland Hotel. We got to be in Legoland an hour earlier than everyone else. I couldn't wait to go on Laser Raiders to ride and shoot laser guns. There were lots of shops full of cool Lego sets. I got to spend my birthday money on Lego sets like Wall-E and Harry Potter. My family are the best. We always have so much fun together.

Carter Franklin Davidson (9)

Cheddar Grove Primary School, Bedminster Down

The New Discovery

Dear Diary,

I am in quite a situation. You see, yesterday, I discovered a new element and now it has formed into a disturbing moving blob. It talks. I'm not sure what to do about it, but I know it thrives in heat. Perhaps I should name it? Steve fits. Well, Steve shall be hiding in my greenhouse for the time being. Though I need to train him not to eat my berry bush, I need the berries to make jam. Anyways, I'd better set off before Steve tears down my wall.

- Marie Curie

Deedee Downs (11)

Cheddar Grove Primary School, Bedminster Down

Effie And The Magic Key

Dear Diary,

Today, a box appeared in my room. It was brown, so I opened it. There was a magic key inside and there was also a piece of paper! It said: 'You have to find the right door for it. There will be one million pounds inside if you find it! Good luck!'

So me and sister Iris set off. It had been ten days. We climbed over the hills and bushes and finally found it! Hooray! What a day it has been. It has been so, so fun!

Goodnight, Diary. See you tomorrow. Night!

Iris Hobbs (8)

Cheddar Grove Primary School, Bedminster Down

Samie And The Vet Surprise

Dear Diary,

It's my birthday and I am twenty-one years young.

Today, I woke up and ate my waffles but then I got a very serious work call from the vets.

Unfortunately, a kitten had a chipped bone in its left paw. I ran as fast as possible so I could save this mini kitten.

To my surprise, it was a planned party with all of my precious work colleagues. The lights were illuminated and the cake was amazing, but the best gift of all was my great and kind-hearted friends.

Kaitlyn Hughes (11)

Cheddar Grove Primary School, Bedminster Down

The Diary Of The Talking Foot Family

Dear Diary,

Last week, I went on a trip to Mexico. I went with my family. It was amazing until a war happened on the third day we were there. We had no idea what started it but we were very, very shocked. We managed to run away and find a getaway vehicle, but it had no keys. We didn't know what to do until my mum found them under the gigantic wheel. Mum drove like a supersonic F1 driver, so it only took 5 hours to get to India. We all eventually got home and felt very safe.

Florence Magor (8)

Cheddar Grove Primary School, Bedminster Down

Eleanor's Happy Day

Dear Diary,

Today, I went to school and I loved it because we learnt how to do times tables in the Column Method. Then I went to my swimming class and we were learning a new swimming technique. It was so hard but I did it perfectly. At the end of the lesson, Hannah, my swimming teacher, moved me up to stage four with two of my friends because we did really good. I was so happy and proud of myself. I collected my new badge and went home to show my dad. It was a great day.

Eleanor Smith (7)

Cheddar Grove Primary School, Bedminster Down

Marcus Rashford: The Best Day Of My Life

Dear Diary,

Yesterday was the best day of my life. I scored the winning penalty in a shootout in the World Cup final in Las Vegas. I saw my parents and my sister in the crowd. I felt so proud. I was anxious about taking the penalty because if I missed, we would lose the game and let people down. I can't wait to go home next week with my confidence so high. I hope I can keep scoring lots of goals for my club. I can do this! I feel on top of the world. I am so happy.

Teddy Horgan (9)

Cheddar Grove Primary School, Bedminster Down

The Magnifying Glass

Dear Diary,

I found this weird item. So, I was in my favourite cafe when I saw a magnifying glass. I picked it up and looked through it. Just then, a dog went past. Yet, in the magnifying glass, they were human. That's when I realised I'd found something extraordinary. At noon, I wondered what a human would look like, so I decided to find out. I looked in the mirror and... *I was an animal!*

Rose Hook (11)
Cheddar Grove Primary School, Bedminster Down

Draco Malfoy's Diary

Dear Diary,
Today, stupid Potter and that Mudblood insulted the Death Eater out of me. Also today, I got kicked by a chicken, *a chicken!* Despite this, I am so joyful as it is the last week of term.

Dear Diary,
I am at Malfoy Manor. The Dark Lord and my aunt, Bellatrix, are here.
Signed,
Draco Malfoy.

P.S. Draco Malfoy is my favourite Harry Potter character.

Daisy Prewett (11)
Cheddar Grove Primary School, Bedminster Down

The Diary Of The Wimpy Kid

Dear Diary,

Today was a mind-blower because my mum and I were going to go to the supermarket to get a diary but she told me to get a journal, so I just went with it. So there we have it, we went to the shop and the man gave me a lucky journal but I didn't believe him. But on the way home, I tripped over and my journal saved me. Thank you for listening. Signed Dexter.

Dexter Cook (8)

Cheddar Grove Primary School, Bedminster Down

Gamer Bear

Dear Diary,

I played a game in the morning for 5 minutes. The game crashed due to network failure. I was so angry I smashed the table and chopped it in half. I then got a new desk and played the game forever and ever.

Freddy.

Sonny Brentley (10)

Cheddar Grove Primary School, Bedminster Down

Young Killer

"Alright, she's escaped... for the 14th time," said the sheriff! She was a dark, mysterious little girl who... was a criminal, perhaps famous for it. Her name is Mistie. She was really only 5! She's done a horrible lot of murders and deaths. She even started a war.

"Quick, the safe is over there!" said Mistie.

She has no parents, people say she's mentally ill. She's normally always busy being a criminal. She's been writing top secrets!

"Okay, it looks like she's on the run," said the sheriff. "A pretty young age for crimes!" Even police were scared of her!

Moonshine Lawani (8)

Colmers Farm Junior School, Birmingham

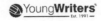

The Mysterious Box

The little well-behaved boy's going on a school trip with his classmates and teachers. In a blink of an eye, he faints.

His diamond eyes gradually open as he regains consciousness in a miniature abandoned house and is wondering, *where am I? Where is everyone?* He hears big, loud footsteps.

A loud voice says, "Don't open this box!"

He faints and wakes up in a glowing, gleaming bed with a mysterious box in front of him. He doesn't remember what the voice said. He opens the box with hesitation. *Bang!* A myriad of evil spirits are released.

"Nooooo!" he squeals.

Sujaan Suva (9)

Colmers Farm Junior School, Birmingham

Her Powers!

December 2nd 2013:
Alice was born. The room was dark, but all of a sudden, a bright blue light shone.

March 9th 2023:
Yawn! What a beautiful morning, time to get breakfast. I am peacefully getting my breakfast as normal. Ah, time to get my orange juice. Why's the cup moving? I'm not even touching it. *Bonk! Bink! Bong!* Wait, what? Then I realise I have supernatural powers... I know I have to do something with these powers. After all, I do have them. *What if someone has powers just like me?* I search and search until I find her...

Isabella Atkins (9)
Colmers Farm Junior School, Birmingham

The Treasure Hunt

Dear Diary,

Once upon a time, there were three pirates. These pirates really wanted treasure. They had no luck at all with finding treasure.

One day, they found a piece of sand which said: 'Touch this sand and you will have 100% luck'.

So the three pirates touched the sand.

Five minutes later, they all started to feel sick and very weird. Five hours later, they wanted to go to sleep. They woke up in the morning and felt very different. They felt very happy and more lucky. They went to another island, and that day, they found treasure!

Henry Riley (9)

Colmers Farm Junior School, Birmingham

The Whale And The Crystal

Dear Diary,
My life changed today! Something big happened - especially so because I'm a whale. I was swimming around my crystal home and I saw something peculiar, so I investigated. I saw bright, dazzling lights in pink, light blue, green and lots of other amazing colours. I was a bit scared. I had never seen those before, but I plucked up the courage and explored. The lights got brighter and brighter. When I got close enough to see, it was an actual crystal! It glowed brighter than the sun.
I'll go back every day to see its spectacular glory!

Phoebe Hood (9)
Colmers Farm Junior School, Birmingham

Why Me?

Dear Diary,

Today, my mum told me to clean the attic because she wanted to make it into a nursery for my sister. Whilst cleaning, I accidentally knocked over a box. As I stopped to retrieve the items that fell, I was stunned by a blinding light. I quickly realised what was shining so brightly; a silver ring with the engraved symbols of the elements in the middle. I turned the ring over and read the words that were imprinted on the back. There, shone the initials AJ for Aaliyah James... One question constantly burned in my mind. *Why me?*

Mianne Montique (10)

Colmers Farm Junior School, Birmingham

Scarley And Megan's Discovery Under The Sea

Dear Diary,

Today was the best day! I woke up with the sun shining through my window and pancakes for breakfast. They were so yummy! I got on the bus to school with Megan. We were so excited about today's trip! We got to school and went on the trip. Guess what? It was under the sea! We made a special discovery. We found two magical hairbrushes. How do we know they're magical? Every time we brush our hair, it changes colour and we become mermaids! Our hair matches our tails! Surf's up, see you tomorrow.

Love Scarley and Megan.

Scarlett Killingworth-O'Neill (7)

Colmers Farm Junior School, Birmingham

The Battle For The Treasure

One dark evening in ancient Greece, I watched three teams go off to hunt for treasure. They didn't know what to do but still headed off to find the treasure. There were three teams: team one, team two and team three.

Halfway there, team three crashed into a rock. So as they'd crashed, they didn't have a ship to take them to the treasure. Team one and team two were still in. Team one got there at the same time as team two, so they said, "Let's give it to team three because they lost."

But instead, they split it.

Alyssa Killeen (9)
Colmers Farm Junior School, Birmingham

What A Week!

This week *literally sucked!* I got into an extremely horrible fight with a savage fox that caused me to injure my paw! I couldn't hunt anymore which was a shame because I'm a working cat. Two mice showed up, I hissed at them out of cowardliness and fear, but they proved their innocence by providing me with food! I was *so* surprised! Why would *mice* give me food? Their sudden act of kindness showed me we could be friends!
Now, we live as one family. Even my owner loves them! Oh Diary, what a week it has been...

Demi-Lea Hodgkisson
Colmers Farm Junior School, Birmingham

The Hero In The Making

Dear Diary,

Today was such a long day. But guess what? I met All Might! Yes, the one and only. It started in the morning... *Thud!* My heart was in my mouth. I'd been accepted. Finally, I could study with all the top heroes. I feel god-like, I know I'll be the next greatest hero with All Might's help. If you don't know, All Might is the world's greatest hero. I want to be just like him. I've always dreamt of meeting him and now he is training me.

Anyways, I've got to go. So save you later!

Deku.

Miracle Laveni (11)

Colmers Farm Junior School, Birmingham

The Invisible Human

Dear Diary,
One day, a girl I know named Lillian went to school and found an apple. She was very hungry, so she ate it. Then she felt sick. After five to ten minutes, she started to be sick. After, she went invisible and her friends wondered where she was. Then she tried telling her friends but they all thought it was a person trying to prank them. Then she found a different apple. She said, "A different apple! Ooo, maybe it might bring me back."
So Lillian ate it. The apple made her even more invisible, so she gave up.

Olivia-Rose Lee Searle (10)
Colmers Farm Junior School, Birmingham

Diary Of A Snowman

Dear Diary,

There was a boy named Jack. He was on a school trip. He was suddenly trapped in an avalanche and turned into a bunny snowman. He could shoot snowflakes. He wanted to use his powers for good, but against who? He might as well train. His smart friend, Harrison, was also good at maths and he was an inventor. He has made a remote-controlled car transform and play basketball. He made a dummy for Jack. Jack shot snowflakes everywhere and made a mess of the place. Harrison put a jumper on and a woolly hat.

To be continued...

Kamaal A (10)

Colmers Farm Junior School, Birmingham

Logmore Academy And Its Hidden Secret

Once upon a time, there was a girl the same age as you or I. She was called Lavender. She thought she went to an ordinary school, but it had a secret. It was magic! She thought it was a very boring school, Logmore Academy. *What a boring name*, Lavender thought.

One day, she went to school really early because her parents made her, and what a sight she saw. There were chairs walking, pens writing letters and trees coming to life. All this time she thought that her school was boring. Now, she thought that her school was amazing.

Thomas George (10)

Colmers Farm Junior School, Birmingham

My Butterfly World

The tree house is finally complete. Exhausted is an understatement. Three whole weeks of finding bits and bobs to recycle. Everyone's asleep. I'm the only one awake, but I've just realised that my friend's woken up too. Do you know I have a pet butterfly? So I visit my parents. My parents are so happy and I am so surprised. My mum has a pet that is unusual and unique. Everyone thinks she stole it from human land. One top tip: people here love bugs. Well, I'm afraid. I just like how they look. Sorry, I have a call...

Kataleya James-Harris (7)

Colmers Farm Junior School, Birmingham

My Adventurous Journey!

Dear Diary,

I went to the park with my friend, Amira. We found some woods where we found a mysterious staircase. We climbed the staircase. When we reached the top, we were in the clouds! We bounced on the clouds and ate them too. They tasted like cotton candy! We bounced onto a big cloud, then suddenly shot into space. We were then floating in space. It was incredible. A star came near. We grabbed it and *whoosh!* We soared through space like a shooting star! We let go and flew safely back to Earth, landing in the park.

Haleen Mickael Azizi (7)

Colmers Farm Junior School, Birmingham

Brooklyn Dodgers

Dear Diary,

I was born in January 1919 in Georgia, America. I love playing sports, especially baseball. When I was younger, I was treated differently because of my skin. In 1947, I played my first game for the Brooklyn Dodgers. Pitchers would throw balls at my head and step on my shoes, but I never gave up. Every time I played, more and more people, black and white, Spanish and Asian, would cheer for me. I helped to change the sport I love and stood up for what's right. My name is Jackie Roosevelt Robinson. I led the way.

Isaiah Hollyoake (8)

Colmers Farm Junior School, Birmingham

The Diary Of A Footballer

Dear Diary,

I am writing about a footballer called Messi. He grew up in Argentina, but his language is Spanish. When he first started playing for Barcelona with Neymar and Suarez, people were saying there was a competition; who is better at football - Ronaldo or Messi? I personally think Messi is better than Ronaldo. Messi has two kids and when Neymar moved to PSG, two months later, he moved to PSG. He gets paid £400 million and he has a mansion. He has a golden retriever for a pet and he has a pool in his back garden.

Kayden Clarke (10)

Colmers Farm Junior School, Birmingham

Why Did You Bite Us, Mean Snake?

Dear Diary,

Me and my parents travelled to a forest and climbed the mountain with a mountain climber one time. We climbed up with safety ropes and when the climber stepped onto the next rock, it suddenly completely disappeared in plain sight and we came crashing down! I was so super scared, but I saved everyone. When we were at the top, we went down a path and we glanced at a snake! It had laser eyes and it was poisonous! It tried to shoot with lasers and poison but they were dodged. The snake failed and we climbed down.

Valentina Kovacs (8)
Colmers Farm Junior School, Birmingham

The Incident... What Happened To Draco?

It all happened when I woke up in the water. I knew I could breathe because I screamed...
After exploring, I met a couple of animals. They showed me around but we met this guy. He was a little older than me but he was really sweet. He showed me more places and we had so much fun.
The next day, I went to find him. He was with somebody else. I felt scared and upset.
The next day, he wasn't there. It's been a month. He hasn't come back. What happened to him? Please come back.
To be continued...

Lola Sinton (10)
Colmers Farm Junior School, Birmingham

The Incredible Diary Of Me

Hello again! Today, I just went to the fair. It was incredible. I saw a ton of things. The things I loved the most were the pigs. They were so adorable. There was a show on which had the pigs in it. After that, we went and got dinner. I had fish and chips for dinner whilst everyone else had sausage and chips. I don't like sausage and chips. After dinner, we went home and watched a movie. The movie was called Little Mermaid. We had popcorn.
I didn't realise the time. Sorry, but I've got to go now, bye!

Paige Dugmore

Colmers Farm Junior School, Birmingham

The World Cup Heroes

Dear Diary,

Today, me and my England teammates played at Wembley Stadium. The game went into extra time, then to penalties. It was tense. I was up to take the final penalty to stop it from going to sudden death. My heart was pounding. I could hear the crowd cheering me on all around the stadium. I curled the ball into the top right corner of the goal. The crowd went wild. My team lifted me up and we were cheering and clapping to our fans in the crowd. Me and my team felt emotional lifting up the World Cup.

Daniel Taylor (8)
Colmers Farm Junior School, Birmingham

A Day In The Life Of Me

Dear Diary,

Today, the big creature tried to wash me twice. None of which worked out. On the first attempt, he tried to put me in the bathtub. As soon as my paws touched the water, I was out of there like a rocket! I scurried over his head to freedom.

On his second attempt, he lured me into the shower with treats. I must admit that I fell for his trick but when the water started dripping from the sky, I darted through his legs and I escaped again. I spent the rest of the night grooming myself.

Kaiden Fitzgerald (8)

Colmers Farm Junior School, Birmingham

The Diary Of A Year 10

In the morning, I got up and my dog wanted food, so I fed him. At lunch, I ate a bagel. I ate at a cafe whilst doing some homework with friends. She was sweet, so I got a hot chocolate.

After school, I went home and made pasta while filling up my dog Riley's bowl. I ate while my mum was out shopping. I wanted to relax, so I had a bath with 1,000 bubbles. It was fantastic.

After, I put on moisturiser and some other things. I got into my PJs and bed, ready to start another day.

Elizabeth Davis (9)
Colmers Farm Junior School, Birmingham

Crazy Space

Dear Diary,

The moment I woke up, I was not at home. I was somewhere in pitch-black darkness. Only tiny stars were there. Then I realised I was in space, safely with my parents and my cat. I couldn't believe that I was actually in space and breathing totally okay, and so was my cat. Even the food was floating. We were 100% sure that we were in space and my cat was meowing so much, I got a meow headache. So I gave him a bit of food and drink. We woke up. Phew! But today is school time!

Danielle Houta Nya (7)

Colmers Farm Junior School, Birmingham

The Lone Tree Outside My Window

I look outside my window and I can see the lone tree. In the summer, it looks warm, colourful and pretty. In the winter, amongst the rain, snow and cold, it looks lonely and bare, with a story untold. I think our trees are a lot like ourselves. When we're in a mood, we're like a tree in the winter, cold and bare. But in the summer, we tend to smile a lot more. Just like my lone tree, we come to life and wake; never thinking it was once sad and bare. Dare I ask? No more sadness, please.

Khaleesi Mitchell (7)
Colmers Farm Junior School, Birmingham

The Mystical World

I have entered the mystical forest. I can smell burning. It smells like bacon, but bad bacon. Now I feel nauseous. I think I'm going to faint.

I do faint, but as I do, I fall into a portal. I am now in a world of creatures! But they have locked me up in a dog cage. There are many humans here and they feed us fungi. They are trying to kill us. It's not my fault that I'm here.

After five days, they've let me out into their magical world. The creatures fill the forest.

Piper Clowes (10)

Colmers Farm Junior School, Birmingham

The Magic Diary Of A Happy Spider

One day, a happy spider was at his home at the airport in London. He was chilled. He ate all the flies and had two friends, Tom and Bob. They're spiders. He attends school in Spider Land. He gets bullied all the time because of his disability, he's missing half an arm. Anyway, Incy is a super cool, funny spider in Spider Land, but Bob's the coolest. Tom always has his head in a comic book reading about Dennis the Menace. They have the best time at school and love their land.

Zachary Page (9)

Colmers Farm Junior School, Birmingham

The Bag

Once upon a time, there was a bag that belonged to Kylee in Year Three. It was on its way to Colmers Farm. At school, it got put on the peg. When its owner came to get her coat for break, her bag wasn't there. It was on the floor, so she picked it up and hung it up on the peg. Its owner went to break and played sharky-sharky.

Meanwhile, the bag fell again. This time, when the owner came back, she froze and ended up leaving it there. At home time, she put the bag on her back.

Kyla-May Edwards (8)

Colmers Farm Junior School, Birmingham

What My Cat Did Last Night

Dear Diary,

Today, I saw where my cat went for the night! First, my cat put on a human suit and ran downstairs. Then she crept out. As I sneaked out of the house to follow her, I lost sight of her until I saw her flying in the sky! As I looked down thinking it was a dream, suddenly I saw something fly across my ears. Then as I looked up, I heard screaming. As I ran to the screaming, I saw my cat helping someone who got into a massive fight.

After, me and my cat ran home.

Isabelle Barraclogh (9)

Colmers Farm Junior School, Birmingham

The Incredible Diary Of Disasters

Dear Diary,

Today was the worst day. So firstly, in the morning, I woke up late for school. Then I realised there was no milk for breakfast, so I had my cereal with water. I missed my school bus, so I ran to school. I missed my first lesson. At dinner time, I got pushed. My lunch went flying everywhere.

Finally, it was time for my SATs results, but I failed. I was very upset when I came home. My cat was missing. It escaped out of the kitchen window. I was sobbing.

Aliza Kanmi (9)

Colmers Farm Junior School, Birmingham

The Life Of Heidi The Cat!

I woke to the sound of Mum opening a pouch of my favourite food. It was a cold day outside. I don't mind the wind as long as I am having fun with my sister, Elsa. We chased each other and explored the neighbour's garden.

As the day came to an end, I trotted into the house ready for my dinner. Full of delicious fishy cat food, I bounced up the stairs and jumped onto Mum and Dad's bed, ready to curl up and watch a film with them as I purred myself to sleep.

Grace Clifford (10)

Colmers Farm Junior School, Birmingham

The Amazing Diary Of Animals!

Dear Diary,

Today, me, my sister and my mum went to the farm. We saw dirty cows, pigs rolling in mud, chickens laying eggs and my favourite animal, woolly sheep eating grass. Then we bought a souvenir each. I bought a sheep in a snow globe. My sister bought a cow magnet and my mum bought a mug with many animals on it. Then we went back home in the car. When we arrived back home, we played with our dog and fed it some dog food. I'll write again soon,

Freya.

Freya Rutter (10)

Colmers Farm Junior School, Birmingham

A New Discovery

We went mining and made a big discovery. We couldn't believe our eyes when we saw it. We dug it up. It was quite hard to dig up, but once we had, we took it into our village to show everyone. Everyone was excited to see this amazing discovery. Once we took it back, we had to examine it to see what it was.

When we tried, nothing came up on the screen. So we went to the science lab to check if we could figure out what it was.

When we did, it was a big bomb!

Theo Grant-Robinson (10)

Colmers Farm Junior School, Birmingham

Giant Georgia

Dear Diary,
Today was horrible! I was walking alone when I fell. I soon got up and started to walk it off, but it looked strange. I wasn't in the same place! I hid behind a tree and giant people walked by! I rubbed my eyes and nothing changed. Then I looked at my hands and they were huge! I screamed and the giants looked back at me. I started to run and saw my feet were big like my hands. All of a sudden, I started to grow until the people turned and saw me...

Charlie Carr (10)
Colmers Farm Junior School, Birmingham

Horrific Henry Wants To Marry Me!

King Henry VIII has just said that he wants to marry me. I was so shocked that I ran, but now the whole of London is looking for me. I thought of a place they wouldn't look, the Tower of London. So I ran and ran. I could hear the guards behind me, so I took a shortcut only my family knew. It was so dark there, I felt sick. But I thought, *what if my head is chopped off here?* The guards left the area. I felt relieved. I guess I will have to stay here.

Iyanna Makarau (10)
Colmers Farm Junior School, Birmingham

My First Train Ride

I was with my family. We were at Birmingham New Street station. I was really, really excited. I asked my mum if I could go on a train ride and she said yes. We then went to buy some tickets for the family and when the train arrived, I was delighted. We got on the train and there were a lot of people, some were standing. As time went by, some people got off at the stop. I saw trees and houses. It was like they were running. My first train ride in the UK was the best.

Sean Pilime (7)

Colmers Farm Junior School, Birmingham

Kayla's Fun Day

Dear Diary,

We went on the most fun day ever. This was to the safari park where we drove around seeing and feeding lots of animals, even tigers! Later on, we walked down to the theme park to sit and have our picnic. Then we went on the rides. I went on a crazy ride. It was so funny because, on the ride, me and my cousin were getting hit on the head. We whacked our heads and it hurt so bad. After, we went home but I went to stay at my auntie's house.

Kayla Astbury (7)

Colmers Farm Junior School, Birmingham

The World's Best Friendship

Me and Tegan are best friends. You could never get me and Tegan to not be friends because Tegan is super smart and me, I'm okay. I am not that smart but I am okay with it. We are friends to the end and I'd say me and Tegan make a pretty good team and I am happy with it. She's my best friend and she's really helpful, caring, grateful and always fantastic. We have a superpower which is love. We love everybody in a friendly way.

Lacey Evans (8)

Colmers Farm Junior School, Birmingham

The Diary Of The Chickosaur

Today, I wait for the portal to open again. I was once a dino but then a rift opened. I went through and then, *bam!* I was half-chicken, half-dino. So I just wait in the spot I walked through. I get lonely sometimes. All the chickens don't like me.
Wait! The rift is open. I'm going through it now. Finally! I'm back where I belong.

Thomas Hayward (10)
Colmers Farm Junior School, Birmingham

The Dream Team

There is a very cool football team. They are called the Raptors. My favourite player is Henry Reilly and he is the best player on the team. When I grow up, I want to be like him. So I go to football training every day, so I can get better and become a better footballer in the future.
P.S. My dad is an F1 driver!

Oliver Cresswell (10)

Colmers Farm Junior School, Birmingham

The Mystery Weapon And Me

Dear Diary,

Me and my pets went on a trip to a forest and we found a mystery weapon. We ran home and put the weapon on the table. My pets and me were surprised. Then I heard a voice and I held the weapon. Lots of trolls appeared and the battle began. We won. The voice appeared again and it attacked us suddenly, but we still won. It dropped a spell book and I found a spell that could upgrade the weapon. Now, I'm the strongest person in the dimension. I've become the king of the dimension.

Gabbi Sipos (9)
Greenfields School, Forest Row

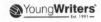

Bob The Alien

Dear Diary,

I went to space and saw lots of stars. It was very dark and the ship was so cool. I took my little alien with me. His name is Bob. We went so fast and we landed on Mars. Then we went to Jupiter in our space rocket. It was very fun, then we had to go home.

After, we got hit by a fireball and we landed in Iceland. But a few days later, an alien from space came to save us. He took us to Spain where we live.

Quentin Garcia (9)

Greenfields School, Forest Row

Me In Star Wars

Dear Diary,

Today, I went into a weird kind of machine and *bam!* I was in the Star Wars universe.

Suddenly, I was in the rebel base and I left for the Death Star but I had to go through about a million torpedo bombs.

Finally, I made it to the reactor and dropped the bomb. *Boom!* The Death Star exploded and the rebels won. Yay!

Ivar van de Visch (9)
Greenfields School, Forest Row

A Blackout In London

Dear Diary,

A few days ago, my brother Jason, my parents, my grandparents and I were having a great time in London. We were gazing at Big Ben and listening to it chime. We loved taking the Tube.

But on one particular ride, the train suddenly stopped and everything went as black as oil. Everybody was petrified. In the blink of an eye, the compartment doors slid open. A man announced, "Don't worry, the train is being fixed."

Suddenly, the lights came back on and the train carried on. When it got to our stop, we got off and left.

Daniel Block (8)

Lady Katherine Leveson CE School, Knowle

Billy Bloodgood's Revenge

Today, I took revenge for my parents' deaths. I am ashamed that I hid that night when the pirates came to the dark, dank Bloody Doom cave and killed them. Their lifeless bodies still haunt me. I lured them back with the help of Steve the phoenix. All day, I was petrified. But as they entered my cave, I remembered my parents' horrifying screams. It filled me with anger. I turned into a vicious, bloodthirsty beast, the side of the Bloodgoods that I have always suppressed. I tore 58 men limb from limb and then collapsed in complete sadness.

Harry Hamer (9)

Lady Katherine Leveson CE School, Knowle

A Day At Caldey Island

Dear Diary,

Remember last year when I went to Caldey Island? I was on holiday in Wales with my sister, Nan and Grandad. One day, as a surprise, Grandad bought us tickets to go on a boat to Caldey Island.

Although the sun was baking, the sea was very choppy and the boat tossed up and down, causing the water to splash our faces.

On the island, we had to walk up a colossal hill to a lighthouse. It was so blisteringly hot, we had to have an ice cream to cool down; I had chocolate flavour - my absolute favourite.

Holly Smith (9)

Lady Katherine Leveson CE School, Knowle

Clean Up!

Dear Diary,

Today, we went to the beach and we went with our Grammy and Grampy. Jamal, my brother, went surfboarding and I made a sandcastle. Then we saw a turtle wrapped in a piece of plastic. Me and Grampy were really sad, so we went to the turtle and took the plastic off. Then we cleaned up as much as we could. Grammy, Grampy, me, Mummy, Daddy, Jamal and other people on the beach we are called the Clean-Up Crew! The Clean-Up Crew are amazing. We cleaned the sand and the sea. People need to keep it clean.

Eadie Hopkins Bird (9)

Lady Katherine Leveson CE School, Knowle

The Diary Of A Wizard

It's been another day at my magic school called Dream. I had to check the Wandering Wizard app on my phone to see what we were learning, it was the fire spell, 'Log'. Aaah sorry, I'm so tired. As tired as a lazy, fat cat. Oh yes, I forgot. My name is Zachaira Foster. Now, it sounds stupid but my wand has got one of the most powerful feathers, the mighty, gold pigeon feather. It cost me 400WC and WC stands for Wizard Coins, obviously! Anyway, gotta go! Professor Knight is calling me.

Logan Jackson-Foster (9)

Lady Katherine Leveson CE School, Knowle

Going To Greece

Dear Diary,

I enjoyed a week in Greece with my family. We had buffets for breakfast, lunch and dinner. They were delicious. Then me and my family went to the pool sometimes. There were two pools; a big one and a little one. We went in both of the pools. Me, my mum, my dad, my brother and sister were in a different room to my loving nan and my other sister and brother. We went to the beach two times and we had fun, but the sand was hot. I collected stones, pebbles and some sand and then left.

Kai Timms (9)

Lady Katherine Leveson CE School, Knowle

Fairy With Koalas

Dear Diary,

Life in Australia is crazy. I went into a forest and spotted a fairy with ten flying koalas. I was shocked because I thought this would be a normal vacation, but I guess I was wrong.

The fairy flew down to me and I said, "Are you a fairy with flying koalas?"

The fairy said, "Yes, I'm a fairy with flying koalas. So, do you want to be friends?"

Of course, I said yes.

Sadly, I dreamt it!

Lucy Faithful-Eagles (8)

Lady Katherine Leveson CE School, Knowle

Animals' Odd Behaviour

Dear Diary,

Today, something odd happened. A bunny and a monkey were fighting. The last time I saw them, the monkey was riding a robot octopus and the bunny was fighting him back with a tree.

This is very odd behaviour for animals. Further reports are due soon...

Aaron Blackmore-Wright (9)

Lady Katherine Leveson CE School, Knowle

The Magic Notebook

Dear Diary,
Yesterday at school, my magic notebook got stolen. Yes, the notebook that helped me get rid of my bullies, the same one that has magic spells. You recite one, it becomes real. I checked everywhere; my locker, bag, classroom, even my wallet, though it wouldn't fit. I knew I had to interrogate people. First, my enemy, Rebecca Ganzeli. She said it wasn't her and swore on her life. I didn't have time to waste, so I asked the boys and girls the same. I asked Emily.
"I haven't seen your blue notebook," she said.
I found the culprit.

Dienaba Drame (10)
Lycee International de Londres, Wembley

My Family's History

Dear Diary,

Today, I had to tell my class about my family's past history and here is what I told them:

"Hi, class. Today, I will tell you about my family's history. Here I go. Hundreds of years ago, my family was royalty and my mother's great-great-grandparents were king and queen. They reigned together for fifteen years. Then the king died and the queen continued her reign for five more years before she died. Now, my family has lots of heritage and they have to go on the red carpet very often. Thank you for listening, bye-bye."

Sixtine Marais (9)

Lycee International de Londres, Wembley

Pies, More Pies!

Dear Diary,

Yesterday, High-Pie sailed away. I was drinking a coconut when I felt High-Pie move. It started softly until the engine bubbled the water. The ride was rough and unsteady. Stressfully, I ran to buy myself an olive and beef pie. The pastry was crunchy but smelly.

Some time later, I saw someone running towards me with pies. How amazing! Everyone knows me because I love pies. Suddenly, the pie seller actually attacked me! It was a bully I had met before, Grogo. He had long hair and big eyes. I needed to run away once more to escape...

Lucile Tse (10)

Lycee International de Londres, Wembley

Blood Shack

Dear Diary,

Yesterday, the most horrible thing happened. Tyler, Lila and I were exhausted after a trip to China and home was five hours away, so we decided to stay in an old shack on the beach. When entering, we found a puddle... a blood puddle. I said we shouldn't worry and just huddle. Then we heard a woman's scream. Blood dripped from the ceiling as we huddled. We hurriedly ran out of that shack. We were about to leave then Lila shouted, "Look!" The shack we saw was gone. We stared at each other in shock: Was it real?

Ayleen Djadel (9)

Lycee International de Londres, Wembley

The One Hero

Dear Diary,
Once, big people were eating us. They came and invaded Earth, they seemed like aliens. They wanted to be more powerful than us, while the humans wanted peace. I was scared at this point, even though I knew the aliens only wanted power. The war began. I really hated war, and so did the others, the aliens wanted power because a long time ago we took their precious diamond by going into a rocket. I had another thought, they didn't want power, they just wanted their diamond so I ran and took the diamond and the war stopped.

Koursami Nasour (10)
Lycee International de Londres, Wembley

Far Cry

Dear Diary,

I am an orphan from Yara. I am very unfortunate because my parents left me and travelled to America during the civil war between Castillo the president and the people like us; poor, without houses, or... parents. The war started because of the Viviro. Castillo lied and said the Viviro was no danger. But we called it poison because Viviro is used on plants. However, Castillo used it on people. Viviro burns and makes you feel sick... very sick. And this is the start of the story about me and my friends surviving the Viviro.

Giacomo Galieti (11)

Lycee International de Londres, Wembley

Problem

Dear Diary,

Today was beautiful. The sun was glistening in the sky and the birds were twittering like never before. And I, well, I was sunbathing on the grass... until now. Now, I'm lying in hospital with a broken leg. To answer all your questions, I will say this. I was sunbathing and another girl was biking, and she ran over my leg. Anyways, that's in the past, and I'm all better now. A full cast on my leg and I've been given crutches to help. I will never go sunbathing again. Not in ten, fifty, or a hundred years.

Violet Le Junter-Sleath (8)

Lycee International de Londres, Wembley

In Poverty

Dear Diary,

Today, the strangest thing happened. A man in a suit said to go to Sydney Opera House and there would be 500K there. So I set off and stowed away until I reached Kuala Lumpur. Then I bargained a ride with a pilot as long as I took up no space. About halfway there, alarms started going off. The plane was going down! So there we were, stranded in the middle of the ocean until Nessie carried us all to Sydney. After a long day of travelling through Sydney, I finally arrived at the meeting site. Then, *bam...*

Malo Laplanche Galton (11)

Lycee International de Londres, Wembley

Art

Dear Nassima,
Thank you for being my friend. I really needed a friend. It is really nice of you to play with me. I love the humour you have, you always make me laugh. When you make a sus joke and you laugh, it makes me laugh. Thank you!

Dear Sixtine,
Thank you for staying with me when I'm feeling a bit sad. You are always asking if I'm okay. It's so nice of you, thank you. I really appreciate it.
I wanted to quit but you guys made me love this school. Thank you to Sixtine and Nassima.
Bye!

Tara Tondriaux-Gautier (10)
Lycee International de Londres, Wembley

The Weird School

Dear Diary,
Today, I woke up very early to get to my new school. I was determined to be early. I rapidly ate my breakfast, brushed my teeth and hair, and set off to school. I walked for about ten minutes and finally got to school. My insides squirmed with nervousness. I quietly entered the normal, grey-looking school. As soon as I entered, the door magically shut behind me! I figured I had just imagined it. I was still quite tired. I walked into the main hall. Suddenly, I heard a loud rumbling and the school started bouncing!

Noah Wiseman (10)
Lycee International de Londres, Wembley

Dystopia 10

Dear Diary,
Yesterday, I woke up to find out I was sitting in a trash can in the rain. I was near an enormous mansion and the guards were looking at me suspiciously as if I'd stolen something from them. I walked off and I started seeing goofy stuff, like flying cars and people with robot heads. I walked up to a group of boys. They said, "Yo, old timer, wassup?" I was thoroughly confused by this. I started asking myself if I was in the future or they were in the past! Gee-whiz! What a weird, weird day!

Gabriel Chevalier (11)
Lycee International de Londres, Wembley

Olivier Back In Hong Kong

Dear Diary,
For the February holidays, I went back to Hong Kong. First, I landed and went to my aunt's place to stay for the week. Then I went to bed.
The next day, I just hung out. I didn't do much.
The next day, I went to a Chinese restaurant to meet up with family. After that, we went to my cousin's place. Then I played basketball with my best friend from my old school. On Friday, I went to my best friend's house for a sleepover. Before we went to bed, we played Minecraft on his Xbox.

Olivier Lo Dromer (10)
Lycee International de Londres, Wembley

The Bloodthirsty Galunt

Dear Diary,
Yesterday, I was walking in the forest near the swamp. Suddenly, a type of anchovy came and bit me! A while after, I felt funny. I started to grow spots and had no arms but more legs. Then my face grew sharper teeth and horns, plus a bunch of saliva. Animals were scared of me and were running away. I had a completely new personality and character. I could run faster and get myself a new live self-caught feast. At midnight, I usually catch myself a little rabbit. By the way, if you see me, watch out!

Romy Pourkauoos (10)
Lycee International de Londres, Wembley

Me And...

Dear Diary,

Yesterday, I went to the park. It was so fun. I played with my best friend, Isaure. Yes, I know. She's called Isaure like me!

Today, I was at school with my best friend and we went to class. We had maths and it was so fun. We got 20 out of 20. I was so happy and she was too!

Two years later, I'm still best friends with Isaure. Yes! I'm so happy because today, the other Isaure and I have our last day of school. We are having a double sleepover at Isaure's house. Yes!

Zoe Guichard Polese (10)
Lycee International de Londres, Wembley

Vancouver Island

Dear Diary,
Today, I went to Vancouver Island to see all of the wildlife there. Vancouver Island is in Canada.
First, I went to one of the mountains. There, I saw a few wild marmots. A cougar was hunting them. I thought he was going to eat one, but instead, the big cat buried it. I moved down the mountain, all the way down to the beach. Two little otters were hugging each other on the seashore. A few sea wolves were strolling on the rocky shoreline. I watched them as they went back into their den.

Chloé Charrey (9)
Lycee International de Londres, Wembley

Family

Dear Diary,

In New Jersey, I was going to school but I couldn't go because I was sick. So I took advantage and went out to sea, it's my favourite place. My grandad told me that the family heirloom is lost at sea. I took a boat and started sailing. When I started, a huge storm started but I still continued. There was a big wave and I sank. My foot got stuck and I was stuck. Thankfully, I got out and got back on my boat. It was the end of the day and I still didn't get out!

Abibah Ka (9)

Lycee International de Londres, Wembley

Alejandro Garnacho

Dear Diary,

I am a top youngster for Manchester United. I come from Argentina and have Spanish roots. I started becoming famous in the Spanish club, Atletico Madrid. Then after a couple of years at the club, I went to Manchester United in my teenage years. I play as a left winger. I have scored 5 goals and have 6 assists in 32 games. I am very lucky to have met Ronaldo and Messi. Me and Man Utd have beaten teams like Barcelona. I am proud of myself.

Ilhan Boulier (11)

Lycee International de Londres, Wembley

The Robot's Revenge

Dear Diary,
Today, I had an anxious, nervous but happy day. I got revenge on the town. Shooting, pushing buildings down on the floor, crashing, colliding, making a big bang! On the hard concrete floor, people were bleeding. Ambulances arrived for all the people bleeding on the floor. Buildings were crashing to the floor. I, the giant robot, was kicking down all the buildings. People were getting killed in their beds watching TV. They tried to call people fast but not fast enough. The buildings fell down too quickly. By the time they were ready, they were already dead.

Flynn Rider (8)
Miers Court Primary School, Rainham

The Amazing Alien Teacher

Dear Diary,

Something happened in maths today! Mrs Wright looked weird. Instead of two eyes, she had three, and she was glowing green! Everyone screamed and ran away, but Mrs Wright was sad because no one liked her anymore because she looked different.

Later that day, Miss Tillett caught the alien germs and grew another two legs! I was in a classroom being taught by aliens! Instead of French, we had Alien. Instead of maths, we had Space Times Tables Rock Stars. Then at break time, they tried to teach us how to fly their amazing, cool, big alien ship.

Chloe Terry (8)

Miers Court Primary School, Rainham

The Sea Monsters Battle While I Am Having Plastic Surgery

Dear Diary,
Today was terrifying. I had plastic surgery on my brain. I was behind a sea monster. I was terrified, scared and anxious. The brain surgeons who fixed my brain told me that I almost got eaten when my brain was getting fixed. Then another sea monster came and they started battling. After thirty minutes, I got some pictures. The sea monster that I was behind won the battle. After the battle, the sea monster smelt me and the brain surgeons and we ran for our lives. Luckily, we survived. I made it out alive and survived the surgery.

Louie Kellow (8)
Miers Court Primary School, Rainham

The Hidden Treasure

Dear Diary,

I was peacefully walking with my parents in the funhouse when I saw a door that I'd never seen before. Suddenly, my parents left me alone. I looked for them everywhere but they had abandoned me. I entered the room and to my horror, the room was haunted. The door closed itself and I was *freaking out!* Suddenly, I saw zombies with sharp knives and they were trying to attack me. Luckily, I'm not stupid. I've always carried gas bombs and was able to escape behind a wall. I could see some treasure. We were rich.

Tanya Chikore (9)

Miers Court Primary School, Rainham

Better Get Your Ring On It!

Dear Diary,

There's a big battle in Australia. There's a bald man, his head is like an egg. I have a few friends to help me fight: There's a fox who is yellow and he has an extra tail and there's a red buff guy with big, strong knuckles.

Suddenly, the battle started. The evil guy launched flying egg-shaped robots into the sky. One by one, they got defeated. They were no match for our teamwork. Then it was just the guy, our enemy, all alone, with no one to help. Working together, we combined our punches to defeat him.

Harry Harris (9)

Miers Court Primary School, Rainham

The Adventures Of Steve And His Companion

Dear Diary,

Before my companion and I set off on our journey, we needed to be fully suited up in weapons and armour. Finally, we were ready to face everything that woodland mission threw at us. Very soon after, we arrived. After looting the mountain, we saw all kinds of mobs. Outside the entrance stood Herobrine. Even though he was so strong, we said we would fight anyone who stood in our way. So that's what we did. We battled non-stop for hours, landing some good hits every now and again. We would either beat the Herobrine or lose.

Dennis Trice (9)

Miers Court Primary School, Rainham

The Way The Security Guard Got Stuck

Dear Diary,

It all began when I arrested a man who stole a rare diamond that cost £1,000,000. Nobody had that much money around here, so everyone was planning to steal the diamond. Luckily, I always caught the thieves before they stole anything. But today, this guy was too sneaky and he snuck past me. Luckily, I got him in time and arrested him. I put him in jail for 100 years because he nearly stole the diamond. I then fell asleep and woke up in a hall of mirrors. I saw a weird ghost surrounding my body holding the diamond...

Ivy Conafray (8)

Miers Court Primary School, Rainham

The Insane Diary Of Lucy May!

Dear Diary,

It's my first day at the holiday camp and it's been *intense!* First, I unpacked my bags and went to bed. The next day, it started raining slime, which is *not* normal. Suddenly, a huge blob of slime fell from the sky, but it could talk! Who knew? Everyone was shouting, so I ran to my room and hid under the bed.

Two hours later, I woke up to find I was in the air spinning around in circles! There was a hurricane outside. I tried not to scream but I couldn't hold it in. *Help me!*

Avani Upple (9)

Miers Court Primary School, Rainham

My Invisible Life

Dear Diary,

I hope my family know that I'm okay! They don't know where I am because a year ago, I turned invisible! At Christmas, my mum made me do all the chores. It made me so angry that I turned myself invisible just to avoid anyone who annoyed me. Of course, now I'm a bit lonely and it scares my teacher half to death when she sees a pen just writing by itself. She thinks it's a ghost. I get battered and bruised by people bumping into me. Well, it's more like some sort of undiscovered, amazing freedom.

Jack Weeks (8)
Miers Court Primary School, Rainham

Steve Finds Anacondas

Dear Diary,

Avoid hippos and jaguars, but I haven't thought of avoiding anacondas. Some of my crew set off to Brazil to find the biggest snake on Earth. Our ten-hour journey was quite long. When we got there, half of my crew were asleep. We all set off into the Amazon jungle. It was beautiful. We could see parrots and macaws. We could see the cold river. We knew that there was a snake in there. A head popped up. It looked like an anaconda's head. Lots of my crew came to have a look. Finally, after forty-eight hours.

Saul Lewis (9)

Miers Court Primary School, Rainham

A Kind Girl

Dear Diary,

Today, I was starting my first day of school and I bumped into a really nice girl called Eleanor. We started going on play dates. We felt nervous at first, but we felt soon a lot happier. Over time, we played together at school and we sat together calmly. We were BFFs. Once, someone tried to upset her, so I went up and got them away from her. When she turned to me, she was shaking with fear, absolutely frightened. I had to piggyback her home. She will always have me and I will always have her back.

Olivia Ranger (9)

Miers Court Primary School, Rainham

The Diary Of Tears

Dear Diary,

I was just chilling in the belly of a whale. I was asleep dreaming of my favourite episode: Series 7 of Find the Treasure, which I've been really wanting to finish for a few weeks but... A *bang!* I thought I was going to die! I said to myself, *it's getting a bit warm*. I thought I was getting cooked alive. I thought to myself it would be clever to look out of the blowhole on the back of the whale which I was currently dreaming in. Then I got discovered and died tragically.

Jack Dodd (9)

Miers Court Primary School, Rainham

The Kidnapping

Dear Diary,

I had the spookiest day of my life. I was walking down the road drinking water when all of a sudden, a squirrel came out of nowhere and stole it. I was furious, so furious that I shot something out of my eyes. It was *red lasers*. I ran home in shock. I told my mum what happened and all she said was: "It was probably your imagination." I rolled into bed and felt beneath me. I saw something. I went below and saw it. A ghost! It started to attack me. I ran. I was getting kidnapped.

Alyshba Bamitale (9)

Miers Court Primary School, Rainham

New Day, New Start

Dear Diary,

Today was an amazing day. We all got told that a new inspector was joining. Her name was Olivia and she was standing next to me.

The next day, she came and met me. She loved her first day as an inspector. I told her I was soon to be a chief inspector. We were sad that we couldn't spend much time together but we weren't going to let that stop us. Olivia and I had the best time together. We laughed and talked and eventually, she started going to awards ceremonies. I was now the chief.

Eleanor Searle (8)

Miers Court Primary School, Rainham

The Diary Of A Ghost

Dear Diary,

Today, I got soaked by a bath in outer space. I was minding my own business floating swiftly across the universe when suddenly, I looked behind me and I saw some fire flying towards me like a dragon breathing fire. I started screaming, hoping someone would hear me but it was space, it was deserted. In seconds, the object caught up with me. It hurtled past me, sending me flying through space and *splash!* I landed in a bath. Soaked through, I angrily clambered out and went back to my home.

Elena Mennell (8)

Miers Court Primary School, Rainham

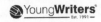

The Talking Pictures

Dear Diary,

Today, I was going to make everyone in my town fall asleep so I could take over the world. Mwahahaha! I did it in my creepy haunted house. I was making a potion when I heard a disturbing voice. I thought, *it's just my imagination*, so I carried on. But then I heard it again. Yes, I am a witch but I do still get frightened. So I went into the living room where all my pictures are. I entered the room and you are not going to believe me, but my pictures were talking! *Help me!*

Lara Taylor (9)

Miers Court Primary School, Rainham

Beautiful Blue Wings

Dear Diary,

Once, I was a beautiful caterpillar. But one day, I was on a branch eating leaves, hanging upside down. Quickly, I felt a sudden change! Something was growing around me, like a shield. I suddenly stopped trying to break free and let it wrap around me... I don't know how long I had been in there. Now, when I escaped, I stretched out my wings. Beautiful blue wings. I started to fly around. It took a few minutes to get used to but when I did, it was the best feeling *ever!* I was free.

Pyper Harris (9)
Miers Court Primary School, Rainham

My Birthday Disaster!

Dear Diary,

My birthday was shocking. I was with my friends outside and a Frisbee went past, so I went and got it. The next minute, I was lost. But somehow, I was next to a rocket. I looked around and I was in space. I didn't know what to do. Next, I was jumping from planet to planet. Suddenly, I saw a glow. I decided to follow it. The glow was getting lighter and lighter. I finally reached it. It was treasure. I jumped on the planet and got back into the rocket. I slowly and carefully went home.

Rose Tingley (9)

Miers Court Primary School, Rainham

Diary Of Garfield The Cat

Dear Diary,

After a late night prowl, I went home and went to sleep. After I woke up, I felt strange. I was somewhere I didn't know. It was a sandy beach. Why am I here? I looked around - nothing. I heard a miaow. A fellow cat! I looked up at the sky and I saw a shining light.

"My name is Theo, this is my beach."

"I'm visiting," I replied.

With that, Theo went for me. I had to get off this beach. I was scared. There was another gust of wind and I was home.

Ella Wolff (9)
Miers Court Primary School, Rainham

The Adventure

Sometimes I just want some different food. Some people just put it in me without even asking me! I warm it for them every night and day without any thanks. So today, I went on an adventure to find tasty food that I like. First, I went to China but I didn't like it, too dry. So I went to Argentina and didn't like anything there either. So I went to Cameroon and I found the perfect thing.
Rumble! I started to go back home and I realised I would have to be plugged in again. Who am I?

Cameron Tharp (9)
Miers Court Primary School, Rainham

Tommy Fury Vs Jake Paul - 26/02/23

Dear Diary,

I won a fight against Jake Paul yesterday. I am super happy and my family are very proud. I partied all night with my family and friends. I haven't seen Jake since the fight. We used to be good mates but I don't think we will be now. After the fight, I talked to him and he tried to punch me in anger! He had disappointment in his eyes. The very bad part is that I have a headache from the fight last night. I am writing this in bed with my baby, Bambi, and my cat.

Tom.

Rose Esme Collins (8)

Miers Court Primary School, Rainham

Game Over!

Dear Diary,

It's game over, I've been caught! It all started when I was in a race. When I came third, I got so angry I turned everything into flames. So the police came to arrest me. I ran all the way to London from Kent hoping they wouldn't find me. I went on the London Eye. I went up so they couldn't get me. They were at the bottom. I saw all the flashing lights. They looked like ants. When I got to the bottom, they caught me. Luckily, someone saved me. I looked, it was me!

Alfie Weeks (8)

Miers Court Primary School, Rainham

Charizard's Diary

Dear Diary,

I had an amazing day. I went to pick berries. Then suddenly, a cool trainer decided to catch me. I did not know what this container was. I tried to escape the scary container but I failed. Then suddenly, I wasn't in the container, I was on land. When I looked up, I saw a creature! I tried to battle but I lost. The trainer told me his name and he fed me. The next day, we practised more. We went to a competition and I won every battle. But I couldn't win the last one.

Dariola Sulu (8)
Miers Court Primary School, Rainham

Diary Of A Flying Worm

Dear Diary,

Today, I woke up in a secret cave behind a waterfall. I looked at my foot because something was wrong with it. I then realised I had one foot and I was a worm, a flying worm! I started lifting when I heard a splash. Then I saw a long snout sniffing around and then an eye looking at me in anger. *Snap!* I woke up in some sort of dark pinkish cave with stalagmites, big ones! And then, well, I realised that I was in the crocodile's mouth and had no clue what my name was!

Josh Thomas (8)
Miers Court Primary School, Rainham

The Strange Man

Dear Diary,

Firstly, I got up and had breakfast with my family. Then a really old man who looked about 100 came and sat in the middle of us with a weird sort of camera. He sat there for a while until his camera worked. He was being filmed, so we all went back to camp. When we got back, we watched him and he didn't move. So we went down to look for prey, but the man followed us. We couldn't find any prey, so we went home to hibernate. The strange old man ended up walking off.

Riley Brown (8)
Miers Court Primary School, Rainham

Tom Gates

Today, Delia was mad. As earlier, I was getting ready by reading my comic on the toilet. I got out eventually. Me and my mate, Derek, walked to school but we were late. Mr Fullerman was mad at me. I tried to do a doodle for me, Derek and Norman's band, but Mr Fullerman's beady eyes caught me again. Next was PE. It was more like training for a war. We had to run five laps around the field, which was so tiring. It was finally the end of the super boring day, so I met up with Derek.

Jack Barber (8)
Miers Court Primary School, Rainham

Murder

Dear Diary,
Today is the worst day ever! Someone actually caught me killing someone. Now I'm in a pyramid but I have a great plan. I am going to kill the guard and escape this putrid place. I'm gonna turn into a scary ghost and get out! After, I will call in an army of killers. *I love my life as a killer!* This is the best day ever. Hahaha! It feels good to be out of that pyramid. I can finally go home. This is the best thing ever. This is the best day ever. Hahaha!

Joseph Hart (8)
Miers Court Primary School, Rainham

The Seed Of Doubt

I was born as a red teddy bear, so cute and fluffy. One day, a girl with brown almost black hair, wearing leopard print glasses and a beaming, kind smile finally took me from the rusty shelf in the shop. She put me in the box and then the next day, she sprayed me on the nose. *Achooo!* She took me downstairs and out of the door. I fell asleep on the way to school. I was handed to a girl with blonde hair and green eyes. It was Valentine's Day. Then I cuddled with my new owner.

Katie Keohane (8)

Miers Court Primary School, Rainham

The Fabulous Walk

Dear Diary,

Today, I went for a walk in a place called Mote Park and I saw lots of friends. My strong-smelling nose smelt something like yummy treats. Once in the field with the grass tickling my paws, my dad took off my lead and I made my way down a hill to the lake. A swan hissed at me and I barked whilst walking away. Towards the end of my walk, my siblings went past on their scooters. At the end of the path, they called me and I went zooming towards them. That was very fun!

Ellie Libbeter (9)

Miers Court Primary School, Rainham

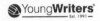

The Girl With X-Ray Eyes

Dear Diary,

For the past week, my life has been stressful. I was with my dad at this place. He said not to touch anything but before he ever got to say it, I went inside an X-ray machine. I love X-rays. It looked cool and there I was, inside one. I sat down inside and it started to go. It was broken, so there was electricity everywhere. It went into my eyes. My dad saw me and rushed me to the hospital. My mum was crying a lot. She could not stop crying until I saved the world.

Joel Olateju (9)

Miers Court Primary School, Rainham

The Living Statue!

Dear Diary,

Today, I saw a victim. It was perfect. I walked up to them but then I paused. I was just about to get her when... *Boom! Crash!* She ran away and put a curse on me. I was sad and I walked through a deep, black tunnel. I started to be nice, but then one day, *boom!* The curse was gone! I was so happy. I learnt my lesson. From now on, I'd be good. But then I woke up. It was all a dream. I still learnt my lesson. I never did anything bad ever again.

Sienna Lynch (9)

Miers Court Primary School, Rainham

The Haunted House

Dear Diary,

Today has been terrible. I woke up in a haunted house and when I looked in the mirror, I was a security guard. I heard a gunshot. When that happened, I was terrified as hell. When I went to explore, I heard a kid scream. After that, it was completely silent. What was it? Will we ever know what it was or will we never know? But after, I saw this weird-looking thing. What was it? I was terrified. Will I make it out alive? I don't know. We'll see.

Lila Stockdale (9)

Miers Court Primary School, Rainham

Life Of A Bear

Dear Diary,

I woke up one day and I saw that I was still on the shelf! Suddenly, I saw a lovely young girl. She picked me up and I heard her say that I was very fluffy and cute. She squeezed me tight and took me to a strange house. It was very loud and the girl had four sisters!

The next day, I woke up and there was tissue paper on my head. I was passed to another girl who was blonde. After, she picked me up and her smile widened so much. Even I was happy.

Maya Cockerell (8)

Miers Court Primary School, Rainham

The Daily Life Of Ghost Rider

Dear Diary,

This morning, I woke up and I was so sweaty. I opened the window. But suddenly, it all went dark. Then I went to get some toast. I ate it. Technically, I put it in my mouth and felt a tingle. I looked behind me. *Oh, there's some dust on the floor.* Then some prisoners escaped and had a fight with my cousin. Let's just say, I put him in his coffin. I ended the day with a bath. I turned on the shower and suddenly, the light went out...

Ashton Bell (9)

Miers Court Primary School, Rainham

The Famous Sadie Sink

Dear Diary,

I have had a very busy day. First off, I had some marvellous pancakes with toffee, sugar and strawberries. Then when I went to work, I saw Millie Bobby Brown with blonde hair. I was in shock. I was so confused, but it looked so pretty. After that, because we're doing Stranger Things, she needed a bald cap. Stranger Things is very jumpy but I love working on it. I need to have a bath every morning for my hair to stay in place. It's very hard.

Sienna-Sydney Dennis (8)
Miers Court Primary School, Rainham

The Squishy Squishmallow

Dear Diary,

I was peacefully sitting while my owner was asleep and when it was the morning, she took me downstairs and played a little game with me. I'm very soft and my owner likes to hug me a lot every day. I got placed under lots of potions and one of them fell! It made me even softer. So when my owner came home, she touched me and all she felt was soft fluff. I'm bigger than I used to be and Squishmallow is my new name. I am as soft as cotton candy.

Sophia Bannister (9)

Miers Court Primary School, Rainham

Snatched By A Giant (The BFG)

Dear Diary,

At 3am, I was snatched by a giant. He was running so fast that my blanket was hitting the giant's leg and it felt like a sack of potatoes. The giant stopped at a rocky cave and he was puffing mightily. Inside the rocky cave, I saw a rocky cavern wall and a shelf with loads of jars. I got scooped up by the giant's enormous hand and he put me on his massive table which meant he was going to eat me now. I was very frightened...

Saskia Bartos (8)

Miers Court Primary School, Rainham

Our Desert Adventure

I woke up and I was in the desert. My dog was there too but he was asleep. There was no water or food. We got up and started to walk but there was a tiger coming to eat us! We escaped from him but we were so thirsty now. We were so scared of him, we walked on. There was still no food or water. I said, "Let's carry on walking."
I hope we get there soon so we don't starve. My mouth is watering as I am so hungry.

Eden-Rose Robson (8)
Miers Court Primary School, Rainham

A Day In The Life Of My Dog

Dear Diary,

Today, I woke up and went downstairs. No one was awake to let me out, but I was very sneaky and cheeky and I used the cat flap. Then I went to meet my friend, Mali. Well, it took her a minute to come out and for five minutes, we barked. Then I went back inside my warm house and napped for about an hour. I had dinner, went crazy and gave Nancy a big cuddle. Then I went upstairs and watched TV and then I went to bed.

Nancy Noy (9)

Miers Court Primary School, Rainham

The Good Diary

Dear Diary,

I get hugged everywhere I go. People love me. I'm always in the mall. I run everywhere I go. So many people recognise me. It makes me sad because I get hugged so much. You might think it's a good thing, but it isn't. I am really nice to everyone, even animals. Sometimes I'm really hard to find. Sometimes my red and white striped jumper gives me away. Can you guess who I am?

Freddie-Ray Kehoe (8)

Miers Court Primary School, Rainham

The Fog

Dear Diary,

I got trapped in a maze! I couldn't see a thing. It was like I was going blind. All I could see was gloomy fog. I had to see where I was going, so I used my hands to see where I was going. The walls felt smooth and cold to the touch. *Bash!* I banged my head on a wall and man, it hurt! I thought I was bleeding but then I heard a noise. It sounded like footsteps behind me.

James Craddock (8)
Miers Court Primary School, Rainham

The Rich Man Who Needed Proof

Dear Diary,

Today, I became the richest man in the world. I don't know how, but I won the quiz I entered one week ago. I'm glad I waited because I won. You needed to draw something fashionable and I drew Air Force Ones. I also own the throne room of a palace. But the government wanted to see proof that I had it, so I sent them a picture of the palace and then they finally believed me!

Ellie Pinkney (9)

Miers Court Primary School, Rainham

The Special Glasses

Dear Diary,

I am a top-class stuntman in the biggest school in the world and I am on a mission to find out who is taking people. I have seen him once, kind of.

I looked for the person but the thief is an invisible person. I didn't know how to catch him but I remembered that my friend is an inventor and he invented glasses that allow you to see visual things.

Isobel Clint (8)

Miers Court Primary School, Rainham

Detective Tiger

Dear Diary,
I had a confusing day. I saw a thief in my desert stealing stuff. I was curious, so I followed him. I followed him for days until he stopped at a car and put his bag with the stolen things inside. Then he walked off and went for a pee, so I jumped in the boot. When he came back, I took my chance. I jumped out and knocked the robber over, then I ran away.

Josh Sands (9)

Miers Court Primary School, Rainham

Giant Baby Vs Zeus

Dear Diary,

Today was extremely painful! I am a giant baby and I was getting revenge on a god in the underground city! The god is called Zeus. It was not pleasant because Zeus is a god and I am not. But two hours later, I ended up surrendering because I got really hurt. So I went back home to go to sleep after the dramatic, dangerous and exhausting fight.

George Baldwin (8)

Miers Court Primary School, Rainham

The Seed Of Doubt

Dear Diary,

My BFF and I were on a journey to London when we got hungry. I went to get food but I didn't know they were poisonous berries. I gave them to my BFF and she turned into a flamingo. She was so shocked. I was so worried. But I saw some blueberries, so I gave her one and then she turned back into a human.

Leila Ware (8)

Miers Court Primary School, Rainham

The Incredible Diary Of Ollie Coates

Dear Diary,
The last couple of days have been out of the ordinary. First, me and my best friend set off on our first expedition. It started off well until waves battered our tiny boat. All hope was lost until we found an unexplored island. Almost unbelievably, we made it onto the island. We could see the most radiant, bright blue waterfalls elegantly flowing down a mountain. Hypnotised by the island's beauty, we hadn't even noticed the *floating island* surrounded by mountains. Luckily, we managed to start a campfire and get some rest.
Write to you again soon,
Ollie.

Adam Coates (9)

St Andrew's Heddon-On-The-Wall CE Primary School, Heddon On The Wall

The Incredible Diary Of Susan Jenkins

Dear Diary,

Today, you won't be able to believe what happened. We reached the island. I couldn't believe the island was in sight. After hacking overgrown branches that sat tangled between the trees, I finally saw the tiny land of gnomes. Every little house was sugar-coated with glistening paint that shone in the roaring red sun. We made our way further into the forest and saw many unimaginable things which no human has ever seen before. I feel truly honoured to see these marvellous sights. I can't wait to continue my journey on the gnomes' splendid, magnificent island.

Belle Todd (9)

St Andrew's Heddon-On-The-Wall CE Primary School, Heddon On The Wall

The Incredible Diary Of Jonathan Zupiter

Dear Diary,

We arrived at the most marshy section of the rainforest of Zublar. We ventured through the harshest weather, causing trouble for the expedition crew. Hypnotised by the wonderfulness and what could lie ahead, we headed over to the ancient dehydrated mangrove. Over the pure, lush, green, dense grass mounds, we looked to see the crystal cyan-blue waters, which were dancing and gleaming in the sun. Looking up, we gazed into the wonderful crimson-maroon patchy mushroom. I recall a fright gazing back into the water because it turned a rose colour in some areas.

Write soon.

Henry Sanderson (10)

St Andrew's Heddon-On-The-Wall CE Primary School, Heddon On The Wall

The Incredible Diary Of Orlando Travelson

Dear Diary,

Here's what happened today: As I entered the jungle, my body was struck with fear as the power of the crystal shard radiated through me. I ventured onwards down the strange blue river, which tossed and turned the boat violently.

When I saw a wooden tree surging with energy, I started until I got to the white speeding rapids... I came to a rocky area where the boat began to fracture apart in the sapphire water. Suddenly, the boat hit a sharp, jagged rock and flipped forward, sending me under.

Talk soon, my favourite book, bye!

Orlando Travelson.

Finn Cassidy (10)

St Andrew's Heddon-On-The-Wall CE Primary School, Heddon On The Wall

The Incredible Diary Of Arthur

Dear Diary,

We were relieved to see the green land and the amazing things about to unfold. We were surprised by the turquoise streams flowing down and the swaying palm trees that danced in the breeze. We were hypnotised by the mountainous cliffs and the dangling down crystal waterfalls.

Desperate to see more of this magical land, we decided to hop over the glimmering streams. We found a ruin lying still on the ground, protecting the temple. I touched the wonderful streams and turned around in delight to see the scary temple again. I wanted to go in...

Talk soon.

Isabella McLean (9)

St Andrew's Heddon-On-The-Wall CE Primary School, Heddon On The Wall

The Incredible Diary Of Maximus Mats

Dear Diary,

When we reached our destination, we saw a waterfall. Suddenly, a volcano exploded and fed on anything it passed. My heart froze. It was ice, not lava. We stood paralysed with fear.

After two minutes of silence, we walked further into the mountains and were greeted by a statue holding a star-shaped wand. Beside it was a tunnel. When we passed through the tunnel, there was a hand labelled 'the hand of power'. It was holding a key. We need to find out what it's used for so we can explore further.

Talk again soon, Diary,

Maximus Mats.

Aaron Johnson (10)

St Andrew's Heddon-On-The-Wall CE Primary School, Heddon On The Wall

The Incredible Diary Of Teddy Davis

Dear Diary,

After a long, treacherous journey, we finally discovered the submerged temple of Zark. Anxiously, I set foot on the majestic island of Zark. Palm trees scattered the island, with rocks everywhere you looked. It was like we were on a dilapidated beach. A liquid carved into the huge rocks.

Next morning, me and my crew got our diving gear ready to explore. As we crawled through the slimy swamp, me and my team saw ruined houses and a huge temple guarded by two statues holding tridents and shields.

I hope to see some more islands. Night, Diary.

Jacob Jude (10)

St Andrew's Heddon-On-The-Wall CE Primary School, Heddon On The Wall

The Incredible Diary Of Amelia Hiland

Dear Diary,
My mum and I went on a boat trip. When we stopped by a waterfall, I gazed into the distance and all I could see was beauty. We stepped on an intricate pathway leading to a floating city. I felt so excited to discover a wonder like this. There were houses of all shapes and sizes. We spotted the most spectacular flower, every petal was a different colour. We were stopped in our paths by a mysterious house. The house before us was most breathtaking and its ornately decorated bannisters and walls resembled a palace.
Talk again soon,
Amelia.

Freya Wilson (9)
St Andrew's Heddon-On-The-Wall CE Primary School, Heddon On The Wall

The Incredible Diary Entry Of Arwen

Dear Diary,

We arrived at an angelic island which had massive coniferous trees that stood as if they were skyscrapers. Hypnotised by the beauty, I could see leaves flowing in the breeze and beautiful grains of sand. We observed a dilapidated staircase leading me to a clandestine basement which stood imminently with cobwebs. Dust filled the air until my lungs collapsed. We came across an old door just on its hinges with a tiny key in the lock. I opened the door and dived down. In the sand, a shipwreck lay with treasure sitting on the deck. Talk soon.

Frazer Blake (10)
St Andrew's Heddon-On-The-Wall CE Primary School, Heddon On The Wall

The Incredible Diary Of Jack Hammering

Dear Diary,
We had made it to the underground civilisation and the last few days have been incredible. I saw a massive opening that was beckoning us to go in. As we bounded through the abandoned crater, I realised why no human being had ever explored this place before. Some bats nearly knocked us down. As we walked, we were halted by a man with a mask and shorts. I asked him why. He said only the civilians were allowed in. Further on, we saw some buildings. We looked inside and everything was mahogany, even the bath!
Bye,
Jack Hammering.

Austin Wilkinson Martin (10)

St Andrew's Heddon-On-The-Wall CE Primary School, Heddon On The Wall

The Incredible Diary Of Lucy

Dear Diary,

As me and Milly were on our way to the unknown land, my eyes spotted diamond blue clouds erupting with brightness. I thought that I was in a fantasy! Hypnotised by the stunning atmosphere of the unknown island, which had emerald green trees in the distance. Frantically, the waterfall made you feel like you were falling down to Earth. As I was grabbing the bags, Milly asked me to follow her up the stairs. Anxiously, I climbed up the humid, lifeless stairs until I was at the top. I was breathing deep breaths in and out.

Talk soon!

Molly Gray (10)

St Andrew's Heddon-On-The-Wall CE Primary School, Heddon On The Wall

The Incredible Diary Of Millie Gronta

Dear Diary,

Me and Billy set off to the Heart of Gold Island. We stole my dad's hazel boat. Billy saw the Heart of Gold Island. After a long wait, we reached our destination. When we got there, the trees glowed up. There were weird creatures. The sky looked like I had gone into another dimension. The moon was out, but there were fluffy clouds. The heart-shaped trees were glowing. There was one huge tree which had a massive path towards it that had razors around it! I am excited to see what happens next. See you soon,

Millie.

Ella Griffiths (10)

St Andrew's Heddon-On-The-Wall CE Primary School, Heddon On The Wall

The Incredible Diary Of Isla Loughead

Dear Diary,
When we set off on our hike, it was strenuous. Certainly amused, I saw a huge snow-topped mountain that looked one million years old. I saw a volcano-ruined house. I also saw a statue, you wouldn't believe it. There were turtles sliding down a waterfall and there was a huge wood. I could see a rare emerald turtle sliding down the waterfall. The day went black. Me and Pepsi were scared but definitely wanted a go, so we tried it out and slid down on the turtle. Then we went back to check where to sleep. We found...

Chloe Loughead (10)
St Andrew's Heddon-On-The-Wall CE Primary School, Heddon On The Wall

The Incredible Diary Of Oliver Darterson

Dear Diary,
The most majestic thing happened; a waterfall formed. It dragged me up it. I observed the creatures. I swam through clouds until an island appeared, sitting on the clouds. I scrambled for land, gazing at the crystal mountain. Water spread out of the bottom. The cave was lit up by crystals. A lush green covered the cave. Animals passed me. I barely got a glimpse of them. The cave went on for ages until it came to a stop. The walls were covered in hieroglyphics. There was no way to the top, so I went back. Bye!

Archie Batey (9)
St Andrew's Heddon-On-The-Wall CE Primary School, Heddon On The Wall

The Incredible Diary Of Belle Clover

Dear Diary,
I stumbled down the last rocks to reveal a gleaming waterfall. Looking around, I saw six targets. I picked up some fruit and threw it at them. I saw a creature coming towards me. I punched and kicked at it but it still got closer. Until it came to a halt! They told me to give them a squirrel. Wasting no time, I passed it over. She handed me a shiny key. Suddenly, her stony layer broke off. My great-great-grandma! She told that she had been stuck like that for over 100 years! Talk soon!

Sofia Robson (10)

St Andrew's Heddon-On-The-Wall CE Primary School, Heddon On The Wall

The Incredible Diary Of Milo Johnson

Dear Diary,

After the disappearance of my dad, I decided to go find him and 60 hours later, I arrived at the fire planet. The floor was magma and after a search, my dad was nowhere to be seen. I then came across another planet. It looked all verdant but still no Dad. I could visualise a waterfall guarded by a skeleton. So I went to that skeleton guarding the waterfall and looked down. To my surprise, behind the waterfall was my dad. I would love to travel with him in the future.

Milo.

Charlie Ellis (9)

St Andrew's Heddon-On-The-Wall CE Primary School, Heddon On The Wall

The Incredible Diary Of Sam Balzorg

Dear Diary,

As soon as we landed, I could taste all of the dust. My body shook when I heard the roar of the volcano. It spewed lava. Me and Dad were thirsty, but there was no water. Suddenly, we saw Buster in the diamond water but we also saw a statue holding a trident. I was so alarmed, I ran behind Dad. We saw mountains with snow. After a quick drink, we got right back to exploring. We saw X-marks, so we dug around for a while but found nothing. I will keep you updated. Bye-bye!

Ethan Grieves (9)

St Andrew's Heddon-On-The-Wall CE Primary School, Heddon On The Wall

The Incredible Diary Of Harriet Walker

Dear Diary,

I was hypnotised by the beauty of this island. Waterfalls of aqua blue sparkled. Where did this town of fish end? I saw the walls of an ancient cabin. Behind me, a shadow of darkness. I had to enter. I decided to make this ruined place look like home. It was a dusty, aged cabin. Clearly, no one had entered for years. Wait! A volcano! It looks angry...

Olivia Watson (10)

St Andrew's Heddon-On-The-Wall CE Primary School, Heddon On The Wall

The Fire Strikes Again

It wasn't supposed to end this way, but I couldn't escape it. Everything had gone wrong. The world was in flames around her. Wait, wait, wait... Let me take you back exactly 5 minutes before this incident... The door of the kitchen barged open, billowing out smoke, followed by coughing. I poked my head in. My eyes widened as I saw the disaster and Bryony shrank back in preparation.
"It is the third time this week you nearly burnt the house down making dinner!"
Soon after, the firemen were called to extinguish the fire. In the end, nobody got hurt.

Elena Swiderska (11)
The Mill Academy, Worsbrough Bridge

How I Saved The World!

Dear Diary,

Today, I saved the world. I know that is super cool. Anyway, I woke up in my cosy, warm vivarium and suddenly, there they were. The pawsome four, my enemies. As a hedgehog, I should have been scared of these gruesome cats. But no, I am brave and strong. Quickly, I accelerated towards them with no second thought. My spikes flew at Oscar (the most evil). Cookie flicked the switch which would start flooding the world with catnip. But then, out of the shadows, Peanut emerged to flick the switch back and Mushev also arrived to defeat them.

Harry Burton (10)
The Mill Academy, Worsbrough Bridge

Rain Player

I was talking to my friends. I had to do my chores. I said I would make Chac do my chores but Chac took me. I said, "Please Chac, forgive me, please!" "Haha, forgiveness must be earned," he replied. I asked Dad, "Please Dada, help me." Dad said no. I found my team; Jaguar, Tree Frog and Bird. The fight started. I scored but Bird got taken down. Jaguar then scored. Chac said, "Ugh, fine! You get water and forgiveness." My life got better. People called me a hero and we got food.

Reuben Rooke (7)
The Mill Academy, Worsbrough Bridge

A Snowy Day

Dear Diary,
8/3/2023. It was a cold, shivery walk to school as snow fell from the sky. I couldn't wait for playtime to make a snowman. Me, Emily and Katie gasped at the snow. We called the snowman Giant. We went to check on Giant when the school day finished. We were amazed that he had disappeared. We thought he had melted until I got home and he was swinging super high on my swing. I couldn't believe what I was seeing. I was puzzled. *How did he get there?* Giant was magic. Today was exciting. See you tomorrow.

Madison Townhill (6)
The Mill Academy, Worsbrough Bridge

I Finally Get Revenge On Pen (Mwahahaha!)

Dear Diary,
This pencil life is bad. You sometimes get it right. Also, Pen gets everything he wants. He marks answers correct and wrong. I get snapped in half, Pen doesn't. Pen is purple, I'm not! I get drawn on by Pen, he doesn't. But I have now decided on something... I'm getting revenge!
Here's my plan: I will take Pen while he is sleeping. I will take the ink out of him and throw it into the sink, then turn the tap on so the ink runs out. I will live happily ever after.
Love Pencil.

Lyla Maggie Dawson (8)
The Mill Academy, Worsbrough Bridge

Pearly Has A Sleepover

Dear Diary,

Tonight, I am going to have a sleepover. I will sleep in a sleeping bag under a tent. My brother Ash is coming too. We are going to have some yummy treats. I picked Haribo sweets and Ash picked jelly beans. We are going to play some games. I am really excited. My favourite game is snakes and ladders. We will watch some films. I hope we watch Lion King because lions are my favourite animal. I will cuddle my toys because they are so soft. I hope Ash doesn't snore too loud. It's going to be fun.

Emily Holden (6)

The Mill Academy, Worsbrough Bridge

Friday Adventure

On Friday, I went for a walk with my mum and my grandad. My cousin, Jack, and my brother, Albie, came too. I saw some flowers. I found some ladybugs and I saw some butterflies. I found some blossom on the trees. There were birds on the trees. Then me, Albie and Jack got ice creams. We sat on a bench and ate them. Mum brought some bread and we fed the ducks. We threw stones into the water. I picked some daffodils for my mum. When we got home, Mum put them in a vase on the dinner table.

Katie Townhill (6)
The Mill Academy, Worsbrough Bridge

Space Adventures

Dear Diary,

I went to space in my rocket and landed on Mars. It was very hot. I nearly melted in my spacesuit. I started walking. I saw something on the horizon. It was green. I was scared but I walked towards it. It was an alien! It looked at me in a weird way. More aliens came. I didn't know what to do. Turns out they were friendly. We played games but then I had to go home. I said goodbye to my new friends and asked if I could visit them again sometime. Today was a good day.

Harper Burkinshaw (7)

The Mill Academy, Worsbrough Bridge

Zombie Holiday

Today, I went on holiday to a graveyard. I was so excited because zombies love graveyards. When I got there, I went to the graveside and I made a new friend. He is a zombie like me. We had lunch together. We ate brain soup and drank blood. After that, we went to the zombie match. The zombies won 2-0. I was so happy. Next, I played hide-and-seek with the ghosts. I think they cheated because they disappeared and I couldn't find any of them. I wish I could stay on holiday forever.

Caleb Burkinshaw (6)
The Mill Academy, Worsbrough Bridge

Dumbo's Destruction Hour

Dear Diary,

Last week, Dumbo drank toilet cleaner. Mysteriously, it turned him into a destructive flying elephant. He flew from home to Wycliffe Prep where Year 5 were doing maths. Dumbo soared through the door, knocking over Edward.

A few minutes later, Dumbo was struggling with fractions. He was drinking whilst doing this and he spilt it all over my work. The class carried on with their maths. Next, Dumbo ripped the electric whiteboard off the wall. Our teacher sent us out for a five-minute break and we played for a while. Maths was exhausting today.

Niamh Pettingell (10)
Wycliffe Prep School, Stonehouse

Rock 'N' Roll

Dear Diary,

I found myself rolling down a hill at top speed! You know when you're in a dream and you pinch yourself? Well, that didn't work for me. As I was rolling, I thought, *how can this be real because I have legs. But I pinched myself, so I don't know, which is annoying.* You may be wondering why I said, "Because I have legs." Well, I'm an octopus girl, so there's your answer. Anyway, back to the story. I was right because I awoke, except my tentacles were dry and I was on the shore.

This is hell!

Lumi Robertson (9)

Wycliffe Prep School, Stonehouse

Slime School

Dear Diary,
You will not guess what happened today. My school turned into gooey, wet, wobbly, green slime! It all happened when I walked my usual short routine to school, but then I discovered my large, boring school had turned into slime! I saw my class standing outside with their mouths wide open gaping at our classroom, which had also turned into squishy, green slime. The teachers were amazed. They looked at the buildings they worked in which were now pieces of slime. The news was on the front page of the newspaper and all over the TV.

Edward Hill (9)
Wycliffe Prep School, Stonehouse

The Avocado Mascot

Dear Diary,

I went home in a shopping bag but ended up in the Gloucester rugby team's changing room! I was selected as the team mascot and led them onto the pitch for the game against Saracens.

Just after half-time, Hastings booted the ball up into the air and I watched it sail towards me. *Thump!* It smacked me in the face.

"Holy Guacamole!" came a shout from the shed. The medical team rushed out to help me and took me to a bed. When I woke up, I saw Louis who was about to spread me on bread.

Dylan Bushell (10)

Wycliffe Prep School, Stonehouse

The Day I Became An Alien!

One day, I woke up and had three tentacles and no body. I went to school and everyone was shocked. I did all my lessons and homework (it was still annoying). Then I thought, *being an alien is not so bad*. I went to bed and slept. I had a great night's sleep. I went to school again and everyone was an alien! We did our first lesson, it was maths. Everyone thought it was boring but I thought otherwise. It was a great lesson! We got to have chocolate!

After the day, I slept and I turned human again!

Lewis Sandison (10)

Wycliffe Prep School, Stonehouse

Gumbo Takes Over Times Square

Dear Diary,

Last night, I destroyed Times Square. It was about midnight. I came to life, so I smashed the glass and grew 250 times bigger. I turned blue and purple. I knew what to do next. So I turned and turned until all the gumballs came flying out. After that, I felt invincible. I heard the police cars coming, so I got into position, ready to smash. I waited and at that moment, I shrunk down and fainted.

I woke up, still blue and purple, with all my gumballs back. But sadly, I was in Gumball Prison.

Frank Carter (10)
Wycliffe Prep School, Stonehouse

The Boy Who Became A Hero

So let me tell you about a boy who saved our city that was under attack. So there was this boy who lived in a hut. He had little money and he was a nice person. He joined the Cyber-Enforcers. Monsters attacked that very day. The boy shot lasers at them, but they were still charging. The boy got his katana and held the fort. The monsters surrounded him. He killed as many as he could and sent a message to the other Enforcers. They got ready for when the monsters came.
When they did, they demolished them.

Sammy Hughes (10)
Wycliffe Prep School, Stonehouse

Heaven's Wake Up

Good morning, my lovely diary. Yesterday was the worst day ever. First, I woke up somewhere different in a place called Heaven. After that, I had a bunch of zombies attacking me. Well, luckily I had a pistol on me. I talked to God and he told me that Hell had invaded Heaven and was trying to take over all of Heaven. I know you think Heaven will win because most people were good in their real lives. But the thing is, when they went to Heaven, all of their goodness went away.
To be continued...

Tay Bigger (10)
Wycliffe Prep School, Stonehouse

Statues

Dear Diary,

Today, I landed the TARDIS in Hyde Park, London. I got out and saw a group of statues of angels near the Serpentine beside a tour. But when I blinked and the tour went away, I was suddenly in the same place but it seemed like I was in the middle of World War II. Over in the distance, I saw a blue police box. But when I walked up to it, it was actually the TARDIS. I went in and went back to 2023. I sent the TARDIS from 1940 back and went to stop the statues.

Brandon Lovewell (10)

Wycliffe Prep School, Stonehouse

YOUNG WRITERS INFORMATION

We hope you have enjoyed reading this book – and that you will continue to in the coming years.

If you're the parent or family member of an enthusiastic poet or story writer, do visit our website **www.youngwriters.co.uk/subscribe** and sign up to receive news, competitions, writing challenges and tips, activities and much, much more! There's lots to keep budding writers motivated!

If you would like to order further copies of this book, or any of our other titles, then please give us a call or order via your online account.

Young Writers
Remus House
Coltsfoot Drive
Peterborough
PE2 9BF
(01733) 890066
info@youngwriters.co.uk

Join in the conversation!
Tips, news, giveaways and much more!

 YoungWritersUK    YoungWritersCW    youngwriterscw

 Scan to watch the Incredible Diary Video